THE ZACH & ZOE MYSTERIES
MYSTERIES
THE SOCCER SECRET

ALSO BY #1 BESTSELLER MIKE LUPICA

Travel Team

Heat

Miracle on 49th Street

Summer Ball

The Big Field

Million-Dollar Throw

The Batboy

Hero

The Underdogs

True Legend

QB 1

Fantasy League

Fast Break

Last Man Out

Lone Stars

Shoot-Out

No Slam Dunk

THE ZACH & ZOE MYSTERIES:

The Missing Baseball

The Half-Court Hero

The Football Fiasco

THE ZACH & ZOE MYSTERIES

MYSTERIES

THE SOCCER SECRET

Mike Lupica

illustrated by

Chris Danger

Philomel Books

PHILOMEL BOOKS
An imprint of Penguin Random House LLC, New York

Published simultaneously by Puffin Books and Philomel Books,
imprints of Penguin Random House LLC, 2019

Text copyright © 2019 by Mike Lupica
Illustrations copyright © 2019 by Chris Danger

Philomel Books is a registered trademark of Penguin Random House LLC.

VISIT US ONLINE AT PENGUINRANDOMHOUSE.COM

LIBRARY OF CONGRESS CATALOGING-IN-PUBLICATION DATA IS AVAILABLE.

ISBN: 9780425289457

Printed in the United States of America

1 3 5 7 9 10 8 6 4 2

Design by Maria Fazio
Illustrations by Chris Danger
Text set in Fournier MT Std

To Hannah Lupica and all the other players
on the undefeated Green Machine,
the last of her soccer teams
I was lucky enough to coach.

THE ZACH & ZOE MYSTERIES
MYSTERIES
THE SOCCER SECRET

ONE

The Walker twins, Zach and Zoe, were on different teams this season in travel soccer. But that was just fine with them. As much as they loved being teammates, they loved competing with each other in sports even more.

Most of all, they loved the start of any new season. It was their chance to see just how good they could be, and how good their teams could be.

Zach was playing on the Bears. Zoe was playing on the Lions. Their first official games weren't until Saturday. So far all they'd done was have practice scrimmages, though the Bears hadn't faced the Lions yet. But their coaches had promised there would be at least one scrimmage between the two teams, and maybe more, before Saturday.

"I can't wait until we *do* scrimmage," Zach said to Zoe. "Then I can show you some of the new moves I've been working on."

"You think you're the only one with new moves?" his sister said.

As soon as they got home from school on Tuesday, they ran out to their backyard and began kicking a ball around. Now that it was soccer season, their father, Danny, had set up a net so they could practice their shooting. Even though neither one of them was a goalkeeper, Zach and Zoe would sometimes take turns standing in front of the net while the other twin tried to score. Danny Walker had always told them the best players were able to pass and score with either foot. Zach and Zoe always made sure to practice with both.

Danny said that was the way to play the game right. By now, the twins knew how important it was to their dad that they did the right thing in sports.

"I know all your best moves already," Zoe said. "You show them to me all the time back here."

"But you haven't seen the ones I've been working on with the Bears," Zach said.

Zoe was standing in front of the net.

"Okay, show me one," she said. Then she grinned. "I promise not to tell my teammates."

"Ha!" Zach said, throwing his head back.

He moved back toward their house then, pretending he was trying to split a couple of defenders as he closed in on Zoe. But as he approached his sister, he suddenly kicked the ball into the air with his right foot, as if lifting it over the imaginary defenders. It was almost like he was making a pass to himself. When the ball came down, he timed his next kick perfectly, and was able to blast the ball past Zoe and into the upper corner of the net.

"Nice!" Zoe shouted.

Zach winked at her. "I've got more where that came from."

They both loved playing soccer, mostly because of how much they both loved to run. Grandpa Richie always talked about what a streak of light Danny Walker had once been in basketball. But Zach and Zoe's dad said that as fast as he had been, the twins were even faster.

They ran around happily now behind their house, all over the backyard, making long passes and short ones to each other. Finally Zach put the ball behind him, as if making a behind-the-back dribble in basketball, and pushed the ball to Zoe, who blasted a big shot of her own into the empty net.

"Gooooooaaalll!" she shouted, the way the soccer announcers did on television. Then she ran over to her brother so they could jump and spin and bump elbows and hips the way they did in their special high five. They always celebrated, no matter which sport they were playing.

When they came back inside the house, they were ready for some of their mom Tess's homemade lemonade. She had left an ice-cold pitcher for them on the kitchen table.

But they noticed something else on the table beside the pitcher and two glasses.

There was a package addressed to Zach that must have just come in the mail. Zach looked at the front and back of the large envelope, but couldn't find a return address. There was no way to tell who'd sent it.

"What's this?" he asked aloud.

"Only one way to find out," Zoe said. "Open it."

Zach did. Inside was a soccer jersey just like the one he would be wearing this season with the Bears. It was white with orange stripes running down it.

Zach held the jersey up in front of him. It even appeared to be the same size as his jersey, with the image of a bear on the front.

"Why would somebody send me a jersey I already have?" he wondered.

Zoe picked up the envelope and looked closely inside. Then she turned it upside down to see if anything fell out. But it was empty.

"Did you leave yours at the field after your last scrimmage?" Zoe asked. "Maybe somebody found it, knew it was yours, and mailed it to you instead of dropping it off at our house."

"No," Zach said. "Mine's upstairs hanging in my closet. Come on, I'll show you."

They ran up the stairs to Zach's room. He opened his closet door. Sure enough, there was his jersey, hanging right where Zach said it would be.

They wanted to ask their mom about the package and the jersey inside. But when they walked into her room, they could see she was talking on the phone. She smiled, pressed the phone to her chest, and quietly told them she was talking to their cousin Anthony, who'd recently graduated from college.

Zach and Zoe went back down to the kitchen to have their lemonade. When Tess Walker had finished her call with Cousin Anthony and joined them, she nodded at the Bears jersey on the table.

"What's your jersey doing here?" she said to Zach.

"It's not mine," Zach said, a hint of confusion in his voice.

"Somebody sent this to Zach in that package you left on the table," Zoe said. "But we don't know who."

"I noticed there was no return address," said Tess.

"So did we," Zach said.

"And there's no note inside explaining why somebody would have sent it," Zoe said. "We checked."

Their mom smiled then.

"You know what this sounds like to me?" she said, glancing at Zoe.

"A mystery!" Zoe cheered.

Zach just shook his head.

"Here we go again."

TWO

Now that Cousin Anthony had finished college, he'd come to Middletown for a visit, and was staying with Grandpa Richie.

"When are we going to see him?" Zoe asked her mom.

"He said he's busy during the day tomorrow, but promises to come by after dinner," Tess said.

"I've missed him," Zach said, shoulders slumped.

Tess nodded. "We all have."

Anthony was the son of Danny Walker's first cousin Tom. Tom had been like a big brother to Zach and Zoe's dad when he was growing up. But when Anthony was ten, Tom and his wife moved their family a couple of hours away from Middletown to Massachusetts After that, Anthony stayed in Massachusetts for college. But he came back to Middletown as often as he could. A big reason for that was his great-uncle Richie, the twins' grandfather. He had always been close to Uncle Richie and was close to him still.

The twins couldn't wait to see Anthony on this visit. But for now, they were more focused on the soccer jersey that had mysteriously arrived at their house. It was lying right there in front of them on the kitchen table.

"I'm not going to tell Cousin Anthony that you two are more excited about your latest mystery than having him in town for a visit," Tess Walker said, eyeing the twins from her seat at the table.

"Not true!" Zoe exclaimed.

"We can be excited about him *and* the jersey," Zach said. "We're just looking for clues."

"And I may have just found one," Zoe said.

Both Zach and his mom knew that Zoe didn't miss very much. Their dad always talked about what great vision the twins had in sports. It was why they were both such good passers in soccer. They were always able to see the field and somehow know which of their teammates was more open than the others.

But Zoe Walker loved applying her vision to everything in her world. Especially when she was looking for a clue.

"We know there's no return address," Zoe said. "But look at the stamp."

"I'm looking," Zach said. "And what I'm mostly seeing . . . is a stamp."

"But what does the postmark say?" Zoe asked.

"Middletown," Zach read.

"So . . ." Zoe began, "whoever sent this jersey to you is from our town!"

She turned to her brother for a quick high five.

"Goooalllll!" Zoe cheered, just not quite as loudly as she had outside.

They all laughed. Zach and Zoe hadn't solved anything yet. They both knew there was a long way to go. But somebody had started this game with the Walker twins by sending Zach this jersey.

Game on.

THREE

There was finally a practice scrimmage between the Bears and the Lions the following evening.

There were seven players to a side in third-grade soccer. Zach and Zoe thought that was a perfect number, because everybody seemed to be involved and they all got plenty of chances to touch the ball. Soccer almost felt like basketball this way. It was as much of a team game as it could possibly be.

Their dad agreed with them.

"The principles in both games are the same," Danny Walker said. "Keep yourself moving. Keep the ball moving. And fill open spaces."

And that's exactly the way their scrimmage had gone tonight. Zach scored one goal, and

assisted on another scored by his teammate Alex Rather, whose dad was the Bears' coach. Zoe scored a goal herself, and also got an assist on a perfect pass to Pedro Rivera. The score was 2–2 when Coach Rather finally blew his whistle to signal the scrimmage was over. At that point, everyone wished they could continue playing.

Zoe gathered with her teammates on one side of the field. Coach Rather called the Bears players over to the other side, telling them he had an announcement to make. He said the coach of one of the fourth-grade travel teams had just been transferred to another town by the company he worked for. The people in charge of youth soccer in Middletown had asked if Coach Rather could move up and coach the fourth-graders.

"But then who's going to be our coach?" Zach asked.

"It's only Wednesday," he said. "The president of Middletown soccer told me they'd have a replacement by the end of the week. Or at least in time for the first game on Saturday. But until then, Mrs. Okafor will be in charge."

Mrs. Okafor was the mother of Kofi Okafor, the best player on the Bears. The Okafors had moved to Middletown from Ghana, in Africa. Kofi said that when his mom was younger, she'd played on the women's World Cup team from Ghana. So even if it was just for a few days, the Bears knew they were getting a really good coach. Unfortunately, Mrs. Okafor couldn't be their permanent coach, because she had to travel a lot for her job. She wouldn't be in town for most of their scheduled games.

"I hope you're ready to run even more than we already do," Kofi said. "Sometimes with my mom I feel as if I'm training for a marathon!"

"The more running there is, the better I like it," Zach said, even though some of the other kids groaned.

Then he ran across the field and told his sister about Coach Rather. As soon as he did, Zoe crossed her arms in front of her and frowned, as if she was curious about something.

"You have a question," Zach said.

"More like an idea," Zoe said, "even though it might not be a great one."

"How about you let me be the judge of that?" Zach said, grinning at his sister.

"Maybe there's a connection here," she said.

"A connection . . . to what?" Zach asked, waiting for Zoe to explain.

"One day we pretty much find a Bears jersey in the mail," she said. "The very next day, the Bears lose their coach."

"But why would those two things have anything to do with each other?" Zach questioned.

Zoe shrugged. "No clue."

"What we need is *another* clue," Zach said. "Badly!"

"Now that," his sister said, "*is* a great idea."

Even though they weren't on the same team in soccer, they were still a team off the field.

FOUR

As promised, Cousin Anthony called right after the Walkers finished dinner to say he was on his way over.

"Maybe they taught him a class in college about solving mysteries," Zach said.

"Don't worry," Zoe said to her brother. "We've always figured things out before. We'll find out who sent you that jersey."

"Your sister sounds pretty confident," Danny Walker said.

"I just like to set goals for myself," Zoe said.

Zach grinned. "And not just soccer goals."

"I want to know who sent that jersey before we play our first games on Saturday," Zoe said, determined.

"Wow," Zach said to his sister, "you don't make things easy on yourself."

"What would be the fun in that?" she said.

After the twins helped their parents clean up the kitchen, Zoe asked Zach if he wanted to go upstairs and take one more look at the mysterious jersey before Anthony arrived.

"You think we might have missed something?" Zach said.

"No way we'll know for sure until we take another look," she replied.

When they got to Zach's room, they carefully placed Zach's game jersey on his bed beside the one that came in the mail.

"They can't just be jerseys with the same colors and the same Bears logo," Zach said with certainty.

Zoe was quiet. She was staring hard, first at one jersey, then the other. She even walked over and switched on Zach's desk lamp, to bring more light into the bedroom.

"What are you looking at?" Zach said.

"The colors," Zoe said, continuing to shift her head back and forth between the jerseys.

Zach looked with her, then shook his head. "But they're exactly the same."

"Not exactly," Zoe said.

She held up the Bears jersey that had been sent to Zach.

"Check it out," she said. "The orange stripes on this one are lighter than the ones on yours."

Zach put his face close to his jersey on the bed, then the one in his sister's hands. He realized she was right. She really didn't miss anything.

"What do you think it means?" Zach said.

"I think it means," Zoe said, "that whoever this jersey belonged to wore it a lot. The stripes could be faded from the sun, or maybe from being washed so often. Or both. Now we know for sure that it's not a brand-new jersey."

"It still doesn't tell us who might have sent it," Zach said.

"No, it doesn't," Zoe said. "But you know what Mom always tells us. It's a good day when you know something by the time you go to bed that you didn't when you woke up in the morning."

"She tells us that all the time!" Zach said.

"So now we know a little more about this jersey than we did before," Zoe said.

"So this *is* a good day," Zach said.

They heard the doorbell ring then, which could only mean one thing. Cousin Anthony had arrived.

"Our good day is about to get even better!" Zoe said, as she and Zach raced downstairs to greet their cousin.

FIVE

Zach and Zoe were only babies when Anthony and his parents moved away from Middletown. So they'd never gotten to see him play basketball or soccer in high school. Those were his two best sports, just the way they'd been Danny Walker's best sports when he was in school.

But when he came to visit Middletown while in college, he was never too busy to shoot baskets with the twins in the driveway or kick a soccer ball around in the yard. Sometimes he'd even pitch them Wiffle balls for games of Home Run Derby.

If the twins were playing any kind of game while he was visiting, he'd always come to watch. He liked to call himself their honorary big brother, and that was just fine with Zach and Zoe.

Now Zach and Zoe came charging into the living room as if closing in on a goalkeeper, both of them hugging Anthony at once. Before they even pulled back from him, Zoe was asking, "How long are you staying?"

Cousin Anthony said he might stay a week or even longer. He was going to begin the job search and try to figure out what kind of work would make him happiest now that he'd graduated from college.

"But you know what's making me happiest right now?" he said. "Seeing the two of you. I can't believe how tall you've gotten."

"I'm a little taller," Zach said, straightening a bit.

"He's not," Zoe said. "He just thinks he is."

Anthony sat on the couch, with the twins on either side of him. He wanted to know all about the Bears and the Lions, and grinned as he asked which team was going to be better.

"Mine!" Zach and Zoe said at once, which got a big laugh out of Anthony and their parents. Saying the same thing at the same time happened a lot to Zach and Zoe. They liked to joke with each other that sometimes it felt as if they were sharing the same brain.

Then Anthony told Danny and Tess that he couldn't believe how fast college had flown by. But he was excited about whatever the next adventure in his life was going to be.

"It's just like sports," Danny Walker said. "You're excited because you know the next moment is the one that might change everything."

"I totally think I'm ready for the next step," said Anthony.

"I *know* you're ready," Tess Walker said.

Then Anthony clapped his hands together. "I think right now, though, the next step should be a game of two-on-two basketball before I head back to Uncle Richie's."

The twins wasted no time bouncing up from the couch and running toward the front door.

Danny, Anthony, and Tess followed the twins outside. Zach went to grab their basketball from the equipment shed. Tess Walker stood on the side of the driveway to record some of the game on her phone. That way, they could show it to Grandpa Richie later.

They split up into teams, Zach and his dad against Zoe and Cousin Anthony. They played the first to make five baskets wins, and it was a tight game all the way through. Zach and Zoe wished they could play all night. But Zach ended up making the winning basket after a neat bounce pass from his dad.

"You're still one of the best passers I've ever seen," Cousin Anthony said to Danny Walker.

"If I remember right, you used to be the same way," Danny said.

"I learned it from you!" Cousin Anthony admitted.

Before he left, Anthony promised the twins that he would definitely be there for the first games of their soccer season on Saturday. It was then that the twins remembered to tell him about the soccer jersey that had just shown up in the mail.

"Well, one thing hasn't changed in this family," he said. "Solving mysteries never seems to be out of season."

After their cousin left for the night, Zach and Zoe went back upstairs to their rooms. When they were finished washing up for bed, Zach went into his sister's room to say goodnight. He saw that Zoe now had the old Bears jersey spread out on *her* bed.

"The orange is definitely lighter on this one, no doubt about it," Zoe said with certainty.

"We already agreed on that," Zach said, sitting on the bed.

"If it's old," Zoe said, "someone had to have worn it a lot for the colors to fade like this. At least a full season. Maybe even longer."

"Well, we always like to wear our jerseys, even after the season ends," Zach said.

Zoe nodded.

"And Dad says the names of the teams in our league haven't changed since he was a boy," Zach said. "But he didn't play on the Bears *or* the Lions when he was eight. He played for the Jets."

"What about Mom?"

"I don't think she ever told us which team she played for," said Zach.

A curious look came across Zoe's face. "What if Mom sent us the jersey!"

"From the house?" Zach said, doubtful.

Zoe thought for a minute. "She could have sent it from the Middletown post office."

"But do you really think she'd do that?"

"I guess I don't," Zoe said. "But we can

still add her to our list of suspects until we find more clues."

"Or we could just ask her in the morning . . ." Zach offered.

"Where's the fun in that?" Zoe grinned. "All we know is that this jersey belonged to somebody once."

"But we still don't know who," Zach said.

Then, in the same moment, as if once again sharing the same brain, the Walker twins faced each other and said, "*Yet!*"

SIX

After school the next day, the Bears and Lions were surprised to have another scrimmage against each other.

On the sidelines, Mrs. Okafor told Zach and Kofi and the rest of the players that the Bears would definitely have their new coach in time for their opening game against the Falcons.

Zach asked Kofi's mom if she knew who the new coach might be.

"They haven't told me," she said. "But if for some reason they haven't picked someone by Saturday, I've told the people in charge I'll be happy to coach the Bears that day."

After all the players on both teams had warmed up with some passing and shooting drills, they were ready to start the scrimmage. But a few minutes before Mrs. Okafor blew her whistle to start the game, Zoe came running over to her brother. She pointed over at Alex Rather standing near the net.

"Look at Alex's jersey!" she said.

The Bears and Lions were all wearing their game jerseys today. The Lions' jerseys were white with blue stripes.

"Alex's is the same as mine," Zach said, without a second glance.

"But not the one you're wearing," Zoe said. "The one you were sent!"

Zach stared over at Alex and knew that she was right. They walked over to where Alex was drinking out of his water bottle.

"Can I ask you a question?" Zoe said.

Alex was one of their best friends from the third grade. He grinned at Zach.

"At least she asked permission," Alex said, smiling.

"She hardly ever does that with me," Zach said.

"Very funny," Zoe said. "Both of you."

"Ask away," Alex said to Zoe.

"Why does your jersey look different from Zach's and everybody else's on your team?" she said.

"Glad the question is an easy one," Alex said, still grinning. "The reason is that this *isn't* my jersey. My mom forgot to wash mine after our scrimmage the other day. So I'm wearing my older brother's jersey from when he played on the Bears a few years ago."

"Yes!" Zoe said, even adding a fist pump.

"You're *that* happy that I'm wearing my brother's old jersey?" Alex said, confused.

Zoe then explained to Alex about the jersey in the mail, and the faded colors. She told him they were trying to figure out whom it belonged to, and why it had been sent.

"Now I know the jersey that was sent to my brother is an old one," Zoe said. "Yours looks almost exactly the same as the one that came in the mail. Same logo design and everything."

"So the person who sent it might not be all that much older than we are," Zach said.

"It's a clue," Zoe said. "Definitely."

"So I helped you?" Alex said to Zoe.

She nodded.

"Think of it this way," she said. "The scrimmage hasn't even started yet and you already have an assist!"

SEVEN

Zach and Zoe's dad wasn't able to eat dinner with them that night.

Their mom said he had a late meeting at the television station where he worked, so she was going to save his food for him to reheat later. This seemed suspicious to Zach and Zoe. Their dad usually made it home in time for dinner. They thought it might have something to do with the mystery. After all, anything was possible.

As usual, Zoe was telling their mom just about everything that happened to her after she got on the school bus that morning. Zach had been with his sister for most of the day at school, and through their soccer scrimmage. But he found himself smiling, listening to all the details Zoe remembered. Sometimes it really did make him feel as if his sister were an eight-year-old private detective.

When Zoe finished by describing how their scrimmage ended, with a great goal from Kofi, Tess Walker turned to Zach.

"And what about your day, young man?"

Zach told his mom that Mrs. Okafor seemed pretty sure the Bears would have their new coach by Saturday, but still wasn't sure who it was going to be.

"You know, I've been thinking," Zoe said, with a mischievous look on her face. "If they can't find anybody, maybe I should coach your team."

"Coach Zoe," their mom said. "It does have a nice ring to it."

"Oh great," Zach said, rolling his eyes, "then she'd get to boss me around more than she already does."

"I don't boss you around," Zoe said. "I just make suggestions. Like the one I'm about to make now."

"What's that?" Zach said.

"Finish your vegetables so we can have dessert!" she said, as she turned and gave their mom a high five.

"Where's Dad when I really need him?" Zach said, and then did finish his vegetables so he and Zoe could have the banana splits their mom promised them for dessert.

When they'd finished with ice cream and cleaning up the kitchen, Zoe said she was going to take another look at the mysterious jersey, in case she was still missing something.

"I just listened to you tell Mom every last detail about your day," Zach said. "There's no possible way you missed anything."

"Even I can miss some things now and then," Zoe said. "Sometimes, when I'm doing homework, no matter how many times I've checked my work, I go back one extra time. I need to make sure I haven't missed anything or made a mistake."

"That's because you never give up on anything," Zach pointed out.

"Neither do you," Zoe said right back.

"It's why we make a good team."

"And why we're each other's favorite team!"

They didn't pull out both Bears jerseys tonight, because they already knew they were different. Instead, they spread out the one that had been sent to Zach on the rug in Zach's room. Zoe sat on one side of it, Zach on the other.

When they were done checking out the front of the jersey, they turned it over, and looked at the back.

"Now I know what Mom means when she says you stare at something so hard she's afraid you might burn a hole through it," Zach said.

Zoe kept her eyes on the jersey. "Somebody sent us this for a reason," she said. "That reason is as much of a mystery as who sent it."

"Remember—it's somebody from Middletown," Zach said.

"Somebody from Middletown who knows you're playing for the Bears this season," his sister said.

"And somebody," Zach continued, "who either played for the Bears or knows somebody who once played for the Bears."

"But *who*?" Zoe said again, a bit impatiently. She'd been asking herself the same question since the day they discovered the package on the kitchen table.

"Who and why?" Zach said. He was as puzzled as Zoe was about the mysterious jersey. Maybe even more. After all, the package was addressed to him alone. And it was a Bears jersey—the same team he played for. It was as if someone was trying to send him a message, and he and Zoe were supposed to crack the code.

Suddenly, a smile grew on Zoe's face. It was a big one, as if something had just dawned on her.

"I *did* miss something," she said, picking up the jersey.

"Tell me," Zach said.

"We've only been looking at the outside of the jersey," Zoe said. "But not the inside."

She reached over, picked up the jersey, and turned it inside-out. Then she began studying every inch of the inside as closely as she had the outside.

Her brother did the same.

"What are we looking for?" asked Zach.

"Something . . . " Zoe said.

"Ohhhh," Zach said, smiling back at her. "*Something.*"

Zoe was the one who spotted it first, at the bottom of the jersey. Written in what looked like Magic Marker, it was so faded that you could barely make it out:

"Flash."

EIGHT

Later that night, Zach and Zoe sat with their dad while he ate his dinner, the words spilling out of both the twins as they told their parents about finding the word "Flash" on the inside of the jersey.

The four of them being together around the table was always the best part of the day in the Walker family. It was happening later than usual tonight. But it was still happening. And because of the clue they'd just discovered, there was even more energy around the table than usual.

"Seems as if we might have two mysteries for the price of one," Danny Walker said. "Or maybe even more than that. Who's Flash? Is Flash the one who sent the jersey? Or is it just someone who knows Flash?"

"I say Flash is the one who sent the jersey," Zoe said. "It has something to do with him playing for the Bears."

"Or her," their mom said. "There are girls *and* boys on the team and, as far as I know, always have been. Remember, I was on the Bears when I played third-grade soccer."

"You were?" Zoe asked, puzzled. She turned to Zach, who also seemed confused.

Tess nodded her head, "I'm sure I've told you that. . . ."

Zach and Zoe shook their heads at the same time. Then they looked at each other and knew they were thinking the same thing. Maybe Zoe was right, and their mom *did* send the jersey.

It was quiet for a moment. Then Zach asked, "Mom, was it you who sent me the jersey?"

Tess Walker laughed, but shook her head no. "You know I love a good surprise. But this time, it wasn't me. No one's ever called me 'Flash' before," she said. "Plus, my jersey didn't look like yours. Ours were brown with green stripes."

Zach looked up at Zoe and their eyes met. After talking to Alex earlier at the scrimmage and now their mom, they knew for certain the jersey belonged to someone closer to their age.

"Now we just have to find out who Flash is," Zoe said, like it was the easiest thing in the world.

"Wait," Danny Walker said. "I know! He was one of my favorite comic-book characters when I was your age. And now he has a television show."

"Real funny, Dad," Zach said.

"Kind of looking for a real person here?" said Zoe.

"You're telling me the Flash isn't real?" Danny Walker said, a surprised look on his face.

"You mean he doesn't have those super-powers?" their mom added.

"Can you two be serious for a minute?" Zoe said to her parents.

"You want to know the truth?" her dad said. "This whole thing is *seriously* fun. And I know that you two are going to figure everything out. Want to know why?"

One more time, the same thought came from Zach and Zoe at once.

"Because we always do," the twins said together.

"Wow," Tess Walker said, "did you hear how quickly that came out of them?"

"In a flash!" Danny Walker said.

"Our parents are *so* funny," Zoe said to her brother.

"They're the ones who should have their own TV show," said Zach.

"Can we have superpowers?" asked their dad.

"I wish we had some right now," Zoe said. "Maybe it would help us find Flash."

Their mom shook her head.

"You don't need superpowers," she said. "Just the powers you already have."

Zach and Zoe went upstairs to get ready for bed. Tonight Zoe came into Zach's room to say goodnight. They always took turns. And this time, he could see that something was on his sister's mind.

"I feel as if we're so close to figuring this out," she said to her brother.

"Dad's right," Zach said. "We will. With or without superpowers."

"But I told myself that I'd solve the mystery before we played our first game. That means I only have one more day."

"Look how far we've come in just two days," Zach pointed out. "And because of finding

'Flash' written inside the jersey, we just scored our biggest clue yet."

Zoe sat down in the chair at Zach's desk, and turned it so she was facing him. He knew enough not to make jokes now. He could tell how important solving this mystery was to her. And of course he knew his sister loved a challenge as much as he did.

"I don't just want Flash, whoever he or she is, to come forward," she said. "I want to solve this on our own."

"I bet you figure it out tomorrow," Zach said.

"Why?"

"Because you're you," he said.

Zoe grinned. "You have a lot of confidence in me."

Zach grinned back. "Almost as much as you have in yourself."

NINE

It was Friday, the day before the soccer season officially started. There were no scrimmages scheduled for either the Bears or Lions, and they didn't practice together. Today was about each team working on passing and shooting and positioning. Even more, it was about sharing the excitement of being this close to their first real game. The Lions took the field first. Zoe ran off with her team, while Zach and Danny Walker watched from the sidelines.

Even though it was Friday, Zach and his Bears teammates *still* didn't know who their coach was going to be tomorrow. It was like a whole different kind of mystery for Zach Walker.

Mrs. Okafor arrived at the field early with the Bears' practice equipment. "Don't worry," she told him as she sat down on the bench. "The folks in charge of Middletown soccer promise you'll have your new coach by tomorrow's game. Who knows, maybe they'll even announce who it is before your practice is over today."

"I'm not worried, Mrs. O," Zach said. "I just like to know things."

She grinned. "That seems to run in the Walker family."

Once the Lions' practice had ended. Mrs. Okafor got a call from her husband. He was stuck at work, and couldn't pick up their daughter, who stayed after school for Girl

Scouts. So Mrs. Okafor had to miss the practice. She told the Bears' players that Kari Stuart's dad, who'd played on Danny Walker's Middletown High team, was going to take her place.

Just then, Zach and Zoe saw Cousin Anthony and Grandpa Richie walking up toward the field.

"Thought we'd come watch your last practice before the big game tomorrow," said Grandpa Richie.

Zoe asked Mr. Stuart if it would be all right if she stayed around to practice with her brother's team, especially since Grandpa Richie and Cousin Anthony had surprised her and Zach by coming to watch.

"I could watch Zach practice with my grandfather and cousin," Zoe said to Mr. Stuart. "But I'd always rather be playing than watching."

"Fine with me," Mr. Stuart said. "You can never have too many good players on the field, even if not all of them are playing for your team."

Zoe, who noticed everything, noticed that Mr. Stuart was limping just slightly. She asked him why, and he said he'd pulled a muscle the other night playing in what he called his "old man's league."

"Wait till you're as old as I am," Grandpa Richie said from behind Mr. Stuart.

Zach and Zoe turned to him and said what they always say:

"*You're not old!*"

The Bears took the field then, and spent most of the next hour experiencing the satisfaction of a good pass or a good shot. They worked on all the skills they had since their practices started last week. When the Bears would do a three-on-two shooting drill, Mr. Stuart made sure to let Zoe be on offense with Zach. It was as if he understood this might be the only time all season when the two of them would actually be on the same team.

On the last three-on-two, Zach passed the ball behind his back to his sister, the same way he had done in their backyard, and she put a big shot into the net over a diving Kari.

Mr. Stuart said they might as well end the day with a shot like that.

"That was a really good practice," he said, when he called the players into a circle around him. "Looks to me as if everybody's ready for tomorrow."

"But there's one more thing we need to do today," Zach said.

"What's that?" said Mr. Stuart.

"Mr. Rather liked to end our practices with one last drill, and it was usually the most fun one of all."

"A game of takeaway!" Kofi said.

"Take the ball away from Coach," Zach explained.

"If we can, that is," said Kofi.

After each practice, Mr. Rather would take a ball and stand in the middle of the field. The Bears would spread out around him. When everybody was ready, Mr. Rather would take off with the ball in one direction or another, and the Bears would chase him and try to steal the ball from him, if they could. It was like him against the world.

If Mr. Rather could somehow manage to put the ball in a goal at either end of the field, the Bears players had to run one more lap before practice officially ended.

But if one of them *could* take the ball away from him, then it was Mr. Rather who had to run a lap, while the Bears cheered him on.

"Are you up for it?" Zach said to Mr. Stuart, forgetting about his pulled muscle.

"No way!" Mr. Stuart said. "I'm not nearly as fast as Mr. Rather even when I'm able to go at full speed."

Zach turned toward the sideline.

"Don't look at me," Grandpa Richie said, holding his hands out in front of him.

But Zach wasn't looking at his grandfather.

He was looking at Cousin Anthony.

"What about you, cuz?" Zach said. "You up for it? You do have your sneakers on. Unless—that is—you think you can't keep up with us . . ."

Cousin Anthony, getting into the spirit of things, smiled.

"I think you've got things mixed up," he said. "It's all of *you* who are going to have to keep up with *me*."

He ran out to the middle of the field, where the ref would set the ball tomorrow to start their games. Then, just to show off, he demonstrated how he could bounce the ball again and again with his right foot, and then his left.

"Uh-oh," Zach said.

"Looks like he's trying to send us a message," said Zoe.

Zach nodded. "We may have our work cut out for us."

"Wouldn't have it any other way," Zoe said.

Zach explained to Cousin Anthony the rules of the game. Mr. Rather usually dribbled the ball across the field until he scored or one of his players stole the ball.

"Everybody ready?" Mr. Stuart said.

The Bears yelled, "*Yes!*"

"Let's do this!" said Anthony.

"*Go!*" Mr. Stuart yelled.

Game on.

The Bears players could see right away that Anthony was much faster than Mr. Rather. Not only that, he still had lots of cool moves that he must have used in high school and college soccer. There was one time when Kofi came in from the side and nearly took the ball from him. Kari came close to doing the same. And Alex Rather missed him by a hair. Cousin Anthony would somehow always get away, as if he had eyes in the back of his head.

He was laughing. So were Zach and Zoe and all their teammates. The parents seemed to be cheering on Anthony and the players at the same time.

But nobody could get the ball away from Cousin Anthony.

Finally, Anthony broke away again and headed for the net closest to where Grandpa Richie was standing. The only players between him and the goal were Zach and Zoe. They thought they had him blocked off. But then with one last amazing burst of speed, Anthony went around them and pushed the ball into the open net.

Then he was the one with his arms in the air, yelling, "Gooooaaalllll!"

From the sidelines, they saw Grandpa Richie cheering and pumping his fist in the air. But it was what he said next that caught the twins' attention.

"You're still the Flash!" Grandpa Richie shouted.

TEN

Zach looked at Zoe.

Zoe looked at Zach.

Zach ran straight for his grandfather.

Zoe ran for Cousin Anthony.

It was as if they were still playing takeaway. But they weren't trying to get the ball now.

Just answers.

"What did you just call him?" Zach said to Grandpa Richie.

"Flash," Grandpa Richie said. "It's what his nickname used to be when he was the one playing third-grade soccer. Didn't anybody ever tell you that?

"No!" Zach said.

"*You're* Flash?" Zoe said to Cousin Anthony.

"Well, it's been a long time since anybody called me that, but, yeah, I guess I am," Cousin Anthony said. "Uncle Richie is the one who gave me the nickname."

Grandpa Richie and Zach walked out onto the field, where Cousin Anthony was standing with Zoe.

"Anthony Walker might even have been faster than the two of you when he was eight years old," Grandpa Richie said. "So I decided to call him 'Flash' like a flash of lightning."

Zach and Zoe looked at each other again, and shook their heads, smiling.

"You played for the Bears, didn't you?" Zach said.

Anthony grinned. "Busted."

"You sent Zach your old jersey, didn't you?" Zoe said.

"Busted again," Cousin Anthony said.

"But why?" Zach said, hands on his hips.

"It was all part of my soccer surprise," he said. "I've known you two your whole lives, so I know how much you love mysteries."

"So now we've solved the mystery of the Bears jersey," Zoe said. "But what's the surprise?"

Anthony turned to Grandpa Richie and said, "Do you want to tell them, or should I?"

"It's your surprise," Grandpa Richie said.

Cousin Anthony smiled.

"I guess this is as good a time as any," he said to Zach Walker, "to tell you I'm going to be the new coach of the Bears."

ELEVEN

They were gathered around the table at the Walker house: the twins, their parents, Grandpa Richie, and Cousin Anthony. It felt more like a party than just dinner.

"How come you never told us you played for the Bears?" Zach said.

Cousin Anthony—or Coach Anthony, which is what Zach had been calling him since practice—grinned.

"You never asked me," he said.

"When did you find out Zach was playing for the Bears?" Zoe asked.

"Your dad mentioned it right before I left Massachusetts. He told me you were going to be on the same team I'd once been on," Anthony said. "That was also when your dad told me that Mr. Rather wasn't going to be able to coach the third-grade team this season."

"As soon as I found out about Mr. Rather," Danny Walker said, "I thought of Anthony, just because I've always known how much he wanted to be a coach someday."

"Wait a minute," Zoe said to their dad. "You were in on this?"

"Well," their dad said, smiling, "I *might* have asked Mr. Rather to hold off for a couple of days on telling your team there was going to be a new coach."

"Does this have anything to do with why you were late for dinner last night?" Zach asked his dad.

"Well . . ." Danny started to say.

Then Anthony chimed in. "The only thing left was for me to find out if I could get a job in Middletown," Anthony said. "I had already applied for a few. But the one I really wanted was an internship at your dad's television station."

"We didn't find out officially that Anthony had gotten the internship until last night," Danny Walker said. "That's why I was late for dinner. I was asked to sit in on Anthony's interview."

"Wait," Zoe said. "You're going to be working here *and* living here?"

"Sure am," Anthony said. "I'm staying with Uncle Richie."

"This day just keeps getting better and better!" Zach said.

"Let me get this straight," Zoe said. "You brought your old jersey with you to Grandpa Richie's house? But what if you hadn't gotten the internship?"

"I'm always telling you two," Danny Walker said to the twins. "Good things usually happen for a reason."

"And your dad's belief in me gave me a reason to come up with this plan about the jersey," Anthony said. "It was really like I sent more than that jersey in the mail. I sent a mystery, too. I was actually surprised the jersey got to you so quickly. I didn't even have my job yet."

"Should have asked me," Tess Walker said. "The mail service is really fast in Middletown. Almost as fast as the Walker twins."

"And Cousin Anthony," Zoe said.

"The bottom line," Anthony said, "is that not only do you two start your soccer season tomorrow, but now, so do I."

"And you're really living in our town now?" Zoe asked.

"Looks like you're stuck with me for a while," said Cousin Anthony.

Zoe looked at her brother. He nodded, because it was a look he recognized. They got up out of their chairs, walked across the room, and celebrated the way only they could: with a jump and a spin, bumping elbows, and bumping hips, as if everything were happening at once.

"Bet even you couldn't do that when you were on the Bears," Grandpa Richie said to Cousin Anthony.

"I'm not sure I could have done that move even when I was in college," Cousin Anthony replied.

"You know what there's never any mystery about?" Grandpa Richie said finally.

"What's that?" Zoe said.

"Who has the best family in the world," he said.

"No mystery there," Danny Walker said.

"And no surprise," said Tess.

TWELVE

The Lions played first on Saturday morning. The whole family was there to watch as Zoe scored a goal and made two assists. The Lions beat the Panthers, 3–1.

"Now it's your turn," Zoe said to her brother after her game had ended.

"Hey," Zach said to his sister. "Not just me. Coach Anthony, too."

"This is the first game I've ever coached in my life," Anthony said. "And I'm just as excited and nervous as I felt back when I put on my Bears jersey for the first time."

"You're going to love it," Danny Walker said. "It just won't beat being out on that field."

"Before every game we play," Zoe said to her cousin, "Dad tells me and Zach to look up in the stands. He says every adult up there would trade places with us, to have one more Saturday morning like this."

"So let's do this!" Zach said.

"Sounds like a plan to me!" said Coach Anthony.

Early in the game, Zach made a perfect pass to Kofi with his left foot, and Kofi scored the Bears' first goal of the season. But their opponents, the Falcons, scored right before the end of the first half to make it 1–1.

The score stayed that way until late in the second half. The two teams were closely matched in talent, speed, and enthusiasm. When the goalkeepers were called upon to make big saves, they did. Zach thought to himself: *This is the way sports are supposed to feel.* One more time, he understood how valuable his dad said Saturdays like this were.

Zach's parents, and Grandpa Richie, were in the stands. Zoe stood next to Cousin Anthony, who let her be his assistant coach for the day. Every time Zach looked over at his sister, he could see that she was into the game as much as he was.

Suddenly the ref told all the players on each team there was just one minute left to play.

Kari Stuart made her best save of the whole game to keep the game tied at 1–1. Then she immediately got the ball over to Kofi, who had a lot of room in front of him to run.

As he crossed midfield, he saw that Zach had plenty of open field ahead, and made a pass to him down the right side.

Zach cut back to the middle. There were two defenders between him and the Falcons' goalkeeper. But then Zach pushed himself into high gear. Instead of trying to get around the defenders, Zach ran straight at them.

Then he unleashed his own soccer surprise, and used the move he'd first shown Zoe in their backyard. It was the one where he got the ball up in the air, over the heads of the defenders, right before he cut between them.

It was his last pass of the game. To himself.

Now it was just Zach against the goalkeeper, with no one between them. Zach didn't wait for the boy to make his move. He kicked the ball as hard as he could with his right foot and buried it in the upper right-hand corner of the net.

Bears 2, Falcons 1.

The ref blew his whistle, signaling the end of the game, and declared the Bears the winners. Zach's teammates congratulated him, but didn't overdo it on the celebration. They'd all been taught never to show up the opposing team, especially after they had suffered a tough loss like this one.

Finally Zach got into the handshake line along with his teammates.

When the Bears were finished shaking hands with the Falcons, Zach went over to be with his family. But as he got to the Bears' bench, Cousin Anthony stepped up and handed him a Magic Marker.

"What's this for?" Zach said.

"After that move you just made," he said, "it's time to write *your* nickname inside your jersey."

"But I don't have a nickname," Zach said.

"Well, now you do," said Anthony.

"What is it?" Zoe asked.

Anthony smiled at the Walker twins. "How about 'Flashy.'"

JOIN THE TEAM.
SOLVE THE CASE!

Read all the Zach & Zoe Mysteries

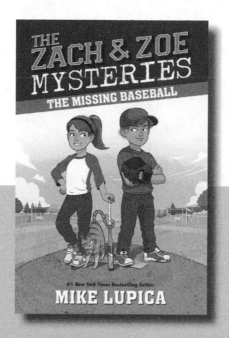

When a baseball signed by Zach's favorite major
league player suddenly goes missing—the search
is on! Luckily, amateur sleuths Zach and Zoe are
on the case. Can they solve the mystery and find
the ball before it's lost for good?

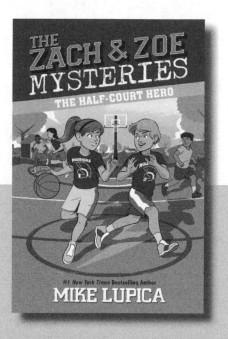

When the twins start a summer basketball tournament at their local park, they can't help but notice the once run-down court is getting freshened up with each passing day. First there are new nets, then the benches have been completely restored. But who's behind it? Zach and Zoe are on the case!

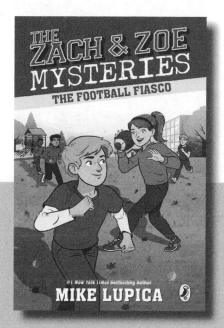

Zach and Zoe are looking forward to their family's annual Turkey Bowl Thanksgiving football game. At school, though, they're greeted with an unhappy surprise when they find their recess football has been completely deflated with a hole near the laces. Who could have damaged their ball? Zach and Zoe are determined to discover the truth!

READY FOR
ANOTHER MYSTERY?

Look for the Zach & Zoe Mysteries:

THE HOCKEY RINK HUNT